Pyotr Tchaikovsky's ballet *The Sleeping Beauty* had been so successful that people begged him to write another. Offered the story of *The Nutcracker and the Mouse King*, he did not like it at all at first. But as he worked, he warmed to the theme – to the musical possibilities, to the magic of that candlelit, midnight world. To capture the sound of fairies dancing, he brought from Paris a secret instrument never before heard in Russia: the tinkling celeste.

In 1892, his ballet was a triumph. It is still a Christmas favourite all over the world. Perhaps you have seen it? Perhaps it will be the first ballet you ever see. But here and now, you need wait no longer for the curtain to rise on Clara's world of magic. Turn the page and embark on a journey, in pictures and words, behind the curtain of dreams, to the kingdom of happiness.

Watch out for the evil Mouse King!

And afterwards, when you dream, listen for the distant tinkling of the celeste and the soft rattle of sails outside your window.

Geraldine McCaughrean
March 1999

For Frances, Christopher, Olivia, and Sebastian with love
G. McC.

OXFORD
UNIVERSITY PRESS

Great Clarendon Street, Oxford OX2 6DP

Oxford University Press is a department of the University of Oxford.
It furthers the University's objective of excellence in research, scholarship,
and education by publishing worldwide in

Oxford New York

Athens Auckland Bangkok Bogotá Buenos Aires Calcutta
Cape Town Chennai Dar es Salaam Delhi Florence Hong Kong Istanbul
Karachi Kuala Lumpur Madrid Melbourne Mexico City Mumbai
Nairobi Paris São Paulo Singapore Taipei Tokyo Toronto Warsaw

with associated companies in Berlin Ibadan

Oxford is a registered trade mark of Oxford University Press
in the UK and in certain other countries

Text copyright © Geraldine McCaughrean 1999
Illustrations copyright © Nicki Palin 1999

The moral rights of the author/artist have been asserted

First published 1999
First published in the United States 1999

British Library Cataloguing in Publication Data available

ISBN 0 19 279969 X (hardback)
ISBN 0 19 272408 8 (paperback)

Printed in Hong Kong

Illustrated by Nicki Palin

The Nutcracker

GERALDINE MCCAUGHREAN

OXFORD
UNIVERSITY PRESS

AT LAST, with a small gold key, Mama opened the door to Christmas. The dining-room had kept its secrets all day long. Now, as the party guests arrived, Mama opened the door, and everyone gave a gasp of delight.

A Christmas tree spangled with candle flames was topped by a silver fairy. Light shimmered along the snow-white tablecloth, glimmered in the crystal wineglasses. Clara simply stared.

'Bet Drossy brings me the best present!' hissed Fritz in her ear. 'Bet he forgets all about you, nah-nah!' Clara sighed. Her little brother was getting over-excited.

Presents lay piled beneath the tree, but Clara hardly dared look for hers. There was something she wanted too much to hope for. Suddenly, she glimpsed them, hanging like peach-soft fruit from the tree – the ballet shoes she so longed to have! She felt like a princess as she tied the satin ribbons.

Fritz jabbed her with a fishing rod. 'Is that all you got?' His tired face was grey, his eyes rimmed with red like a rat.

'It's past your bedtime,' said Clara gently.

'Not till Drossy comes!'

The clock began to strike — that odd, ugly clock carved by their godfather. The carved owl perched on top flapped its wings and spun its head as the hour struck: *Dong! Dong!* Suddenly, all the gas lamps went out.

A wintry wind scuttered through the room, and something flapped past the ladies' bare shoulders. Little children squealed with fright. Then the lights sprang up again…and there stood Drosselmeyer, the children's godfather, midnight blue in his long cloak, wild white hair trapped within a spindle-spired glass wig.

'Drossy! You and your fooling!' scolded Mama, laughing.

For Fritz and Clara, the most important guest had arrived. Each year, Drossy brought Christmas with him, in a bulging, rattling, ancient bag. Through the moth-holes shone bright paint and shiny silver — wonderful hand-made toys. For Drosselmeyer was a toymaker.

'Give, give, give!' demanded Fritz, pulling at the bag.

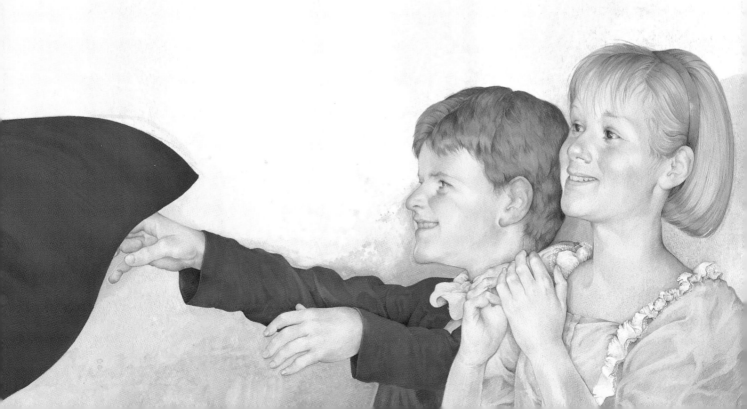

'Permit me to introduce my young nephew, Gunther,' said Drossy, and Clara curtsied politely. Gunther bowed and kissed her hand. Kissed it! As if she were a grown-up lady! He had a kind face, brown-eyed, with smiles hiding here and there.

'What about my presents?' Fritz whined, and finally Drossy opened the sack. Out came a sword, its blade curved like a harvest moon. 'A sword for me!' cried Fritz and shook it in Clara's face. Out came a gold crown with glass jewels and a velvet cap. 'A crown for me!' cried Fritz, throwing aside the sword. Out came a box of lead soldiers, each with a cockaded hat. 'Toy soldiers for me!' cried Fritz, and tipped them on the floor.

'And now, my little Clara…' said Drossy, delving deep into the bag, '…meet Captain Krak von Nuttenkopf of the Queen's Own Regiment!'

Out came the carving of a man. His red uniform was so glossy that the paint almost looked wet. His sword glittered, his black boots shone. His head was enormous and comical, with a big lop jaw swinging open and shut. When Drossy lifted the flaps of the carved scarlet jacket, the mouth smiled open. When he tucked the jacket down, the mouth shut with a snap. Gunther popped a walnut into the soldier's mouth. *Krak!* Out came the nut, and two half shells.

'Oh, he's fine!' exclaimed Clara. 'Thank you, Godfather!'

'A nutcracker for me!' shrieked Fritz. He snatched the doll, wrenched it open and pushed into the mouth a toffee and a marble.

'Oh no!' cried Clara. 'Please!'

Krak!

Fritz turned white, then blushed red. Then he threw the nutcracker to the floor, blurting, 'Stupid toy!', and ran out of the room. Clara picked up her little man. The wooden jaw sagged, broken. Tears scalded her cheeks.

'Here, let me bandage his head,' said a kind voice, and Gunther was there; tying a handkerchief round the broken toy. Together they laid the captain in a doll's cradle, but anyone could see he was grievously wounded. The tears in Clara's eyes turned the candles on the Christmas tree to stars.

'Shall we begin the dancing, you and I?' whispered Gunther comfortingly. So Gunther and Clara danced, and the evening wore away, while Christmas gathered in soft, grey snowclouds over the house, hiding a midnight moon.

The guests were gone. The music was silent. The candles were out, and the dining-room full of shadows. But Clara could not sleep. She stood in her nightdress, still wearing her ballet shoes, gazing down at the poor wounded nutcracker.

What was that? Only the tree rustling its pine needles.

No! There it was again! Mice?

No! Rats!

Clara leapt on to the sofa and tucked her feet into her nightdress. Out from behind the fire grate came a whole swarm, an army of rats! They were led by one far larger than the rest. Bigger than any cat or dog, he wore a gold crown and brandished a cutlass with a blade like the harvest moon.

'To arms, men! The enemy is coming!'

Out of his cradle leapt Captain Krak von Nuttenkopf. He still wore his bandage, but rakishly now, round his brow. 'For the queen!' he cried, mustering the scattered toy soldiers.

'For the queen and Prince Krak!' cried the soldiers.

They were hugely outnumbered; the rats swarmed over them. But Captain Krak leapt on to the piano stool and pointed his sabre at King Rat. 'I am for you, sir!'

How they fought! – hand-to-hand, chest-to-chest, blades clattering overhead! King Rat was strong. Pushing his sharp nose and red-rimmed eyes close to Krak's face, he spat. The captain, still weak from his wounds, fell back a step or two, his spurs caught in the carpet fringe, and he crashed down on his back!

'Stupid toy!' sneered King Rat, and raised his sword for the kill.

Quick as thought, Clara pulled off one slipper and threw it. The gold crown spun away. King Rat clutched his head and sprawled headlong into the prickly Christmas tree. As his troops grabbed hold of a foot, an ear, a tail to carry him away, the tree baubles above jingled like victory bells.

'How can I ever thank you?' said Captain Krak, getting to his feet. He fetched King Rat's crown from the grate and presented it to Clara, bowing very low. 'You saved my life and turned the battle! The queen will wish to thank you.'

'*The queen?!*'

'My mother, yes. Queen of the Land of Sweets. You will come there with me, won't you? And help us celebrate the defeat of the rats?' Clara saw that his limbs were no longer wooden, his face no longer lop-jawed, but handsome, brown-eyed, with smiles hiding here and there.

He drew the heavy dining-room curtains. Outside, the snow was just starting to fall, and there, in a river of starlight, a boat tugged at its moorings. Captain Krak hung his jacket round Clara's shoulders. Then they stepped aboard.

Over a sea of junket, through warm blizzards of sherbet, beneath candy constellations they sailed, to the harbour of Yum. There, lining the waterfront, were toys and gingerbread men, fairies and jelly bears, all waving and cheering and shouting Clara's name. News of the victory had sped ahead of the ship.

'Bravo, Prince Krak! Hail, Miss Clara! Welcome home!'

Welcome home! said the banners.

'Welcome to you both!' said a fairy in a gauzy, spangled dress. 'I saw everything. You were very brave, my dears.'

'Saw? How did you see?' asked Clara, though the fairy did look somehow familiar.

'From the top of the Christmas tree, of course! Come this way. The queen is longing to meet you.'

They gave Clara such a day as she had never seen, such a day as there has never been. They sat her down to a feast and, while she drank from a golden goblet, entertained her with a carnival ballet.

Then the Prince led Clara on to the lemon-ice floor. It was as if they had danced a thousand times before, as if they had danced together down centuries of daydreams.

As the last notes died away, and the last puff of icing sugar settled, the Christmas fairy asked Clara, 'Will you stay and spend Christmas with us?'

'Christmas! I'd forgotten!' gasped Clara. 'Mama! Papa! Fritz! No, no…
I must get home by morning!'

'Then come again,' said the queen. '*Bonbon voyage.*'

The walnut ship sailed beneath clouds of candyfloss, through ice-cream
floes towards the shores of morning. Clara did not feel the cold. In fact, she felt
so warm and contented that she dozed.

While she slept, Prince Krak must have moored outside her window,
carried her gently in, and laid her on the sofa. For when she woke, that was
where she found herself, alone.

Drossy's clock was striking seven. Seven o'clock on Christmas morning. Jumping up, she ran to the toy cradle under the tree. The nutcracker-doll inside it was mended. Someone had mended him! Clara cradled the soldier in her arms and danced about the room. 'Next year!' she told him. 'I'll come back with you next year!'

Each night, the wooden nutcracker stood beside Clara's bed, to guard her while she slept. Fritz never so much as went near it again – as if somehow it frightened him.

But Clara did not go back to the Land of Sweets, after all. The young man Gunther came to visit again, the following Christmas. Clara danced with him at the Christmas Eve party. And somehow, as they danced, the night simply slipped away, leaving no thought of sweets or magic, no time for other voyages.